The Happily Ever Afternoon

Written by
Sharon Jennings

Illustrated by
Ron Lightburn

Annick Press
Toronto • New York • Vancouver

Design: Sheryl Shapiro

Annick Press Ltd.

We acknowledge the support of the Canada Council for the Arts, the Ontario Arts Council, and the Government of Canada through the Book Publishing Industry Development Program (BPIDP) for our publishing activities.

Cataloging in Publication

Jennings, Sharon
The happily ever afternoon / Sharon Jennings ; illustrated by Ron Lightburn.

ISBN-13: 978-1-55037-945-7 (bound)
ISBN-10: 1-55037-945-3 (bound)
ISBN-13: 978-1-55037-944-0 (pbk.)
ISBN-10: 1-55037-944-5 (pbk.)

I. Lightburn, Ron II. Title.

PS8569.E563H36 2006 jC813'.54 C2005-905528-6

The art in this book was rendered in oil paint on 300 lb. paper.
The text was typeset in Postino Italic.

Distributed in Canada by:
Firefly Books Ltd.
66 Leek Crescent
Richmond Hill, ON
L4B 1H1

Published in the U.S.A. by:
Annick Press (U.S.) Ltd.
Distributed in the U.S.A. by:
Firefly Books (U.S.) Inc.
P.O. Box 1338
Ellicott Station
Buffalo, NY 14205

Printed in China.

Visit us at: www.annickpress.com

To Morgan Goodfellow and
Duncan Zayachkowski
—S.J.

Our hero in the story is riding his tricycle in the safety of his own grassy fenced-in back yard. Although young children are not legally obligated to wear helmets while riding a tricycle, we encourage parents to ensure they wear them when out riding.

Once upon a time,

and far, far away,

there was a room
full of treasure,

guarded by ferocious dragons.

No one ever got by these terrible monsters.

No one ever avoided capture.

To be cast into the dungeon was a lonely and terrible doom!

But with a little trickery

and the weaving of a spell,

escape was possible for the
clever and courageous.

And so it seemed that the brave hero had conquered all.

But then came ...

what looked like ...

... the end.

Happily, it wasn't.